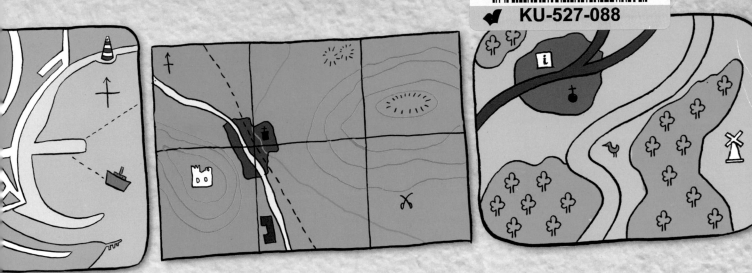

Mapping
where
People Work

Written by **Jen Green**

Illustrated by **Sarah Horne**

First published in 2015 by Wayland
Copyright © Wayland 2015

Wayland
338 Euston Road
London NW1 3BH

Wayland Australia
Level 17/207 Kent Street
Sydney, NSW 2000

Series editor: Victoria Brooker
Editor: Carron Brown
Designer: Krina Patel

Dewey number: 526-dc23

ISBN 978 0 7502 8576 6

Printed in China

10 9 8 7 6 5 4 3 2 1

Picture acknowledgements
Front cover: top centre Getty Images; bottom centre REX/Invicta Kent Media. Back cover top left REX/
Haydn West; centre right Chris Howes/Wild Places Photography/Alamy. Pages: 5 REX/Invicta Kent Media;
7 left REX/Haydn West; 7 right Skyscan.co.uk; 9 Shutterstock/Bikeworldtravel; 13 left Shutterstock/jennyt;
13 right Shutterstock/Monkey Business Images; 19 Chris Howes/Wild Places Photography/Alamy; 20 Getty
Images; 23 John Warburton-Lee/Getty Images; 27 Steven Rollings/Getty Images; 29 Topfoto.co.uk.

Wayland is a division of Hachette Children's Books, an Hachette UK company
www.hachette.co.uk

Contents

VIEW FROM THE AIR

Joe Williams is an airline pilot. He flies passengers between London and the French city of Paris.

The map below shows my route.

London

Paris

Have you ever travelled by plane? If you look out of a plane window, you can see towns and countryside far below. Things look very different from the air. The view from a plane, called an aerial view, is the same as the view shown on maps.

What are maps?

Maps are drawings of the landscape seen from above. Maps contain all sorts of useful information about people and places. Many people, including airline pilots, use maps in their daily work.

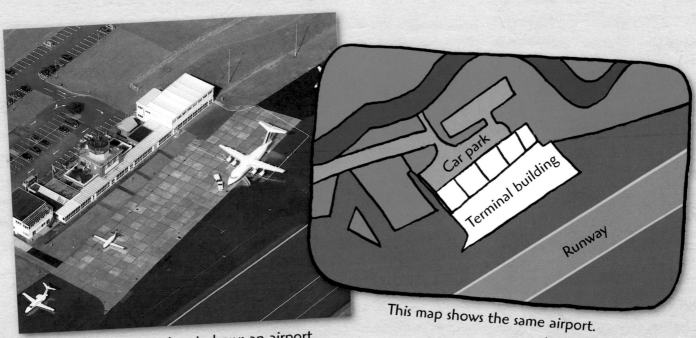

This photo from the air shows an airport.

Car park

Terminal building

Runway

This map shows the same airport.

TRY THIS!

To read and make maps you have to get used to seeing things from above. Practise drawing landmarks, such as these buildings, from above.

POST PERSON'S ROUND

Shirley Woods is a postwoman. She delivers mail in a small town.

The map below, called a street map, shows my delivery area.

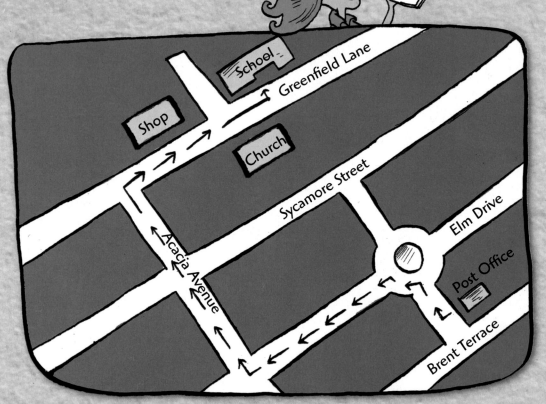

Street maps are used to find the way in towns and cities.

Street maps

Street maps show part of a city or town in detail, including street names. Delivery people like Shirley use street maps to get to know the area. They need to know the location of every house, so they don't miss anyone out!

Finding the way

High walls and hedges hide some houses from the road. But the aerial view of the map shows things that can't be seen at ground level. This viewpoint also shows if places are close together or far apart, and whether you need to turn left, right or go straight on to get to where you want to go.

A postwoman on her bike.

This photo shows streets from above.

TRY THIS!

Look at the map opposite and answer these questions:

- What landmarks are shown on Greenfield Lane?
- In which direction does Shirley turn to get from Acacia Avenue into Greenfield Lane?

CITY GUIDE'S MAP

James Garvey works as a tour guide. He guides tourists around London and tells people about the city's history. Before the tour starts, James hands out tourist maps, so everyone can see the route.

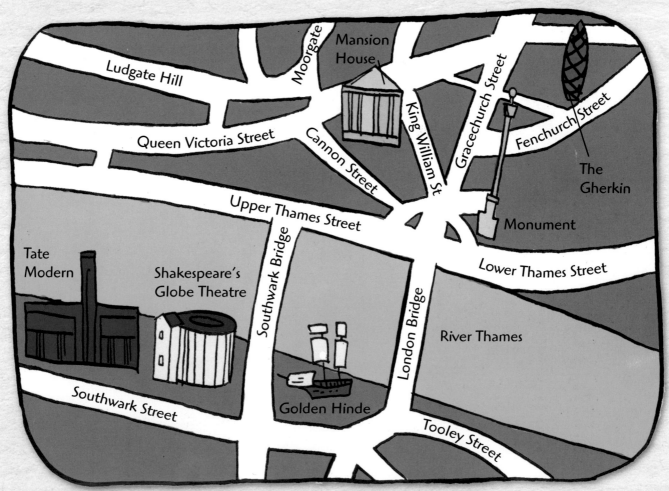

This map shows the City of London.

Tourist maps

Tourist maps show the famous sights of a city. Churches, palaces, statues and bridges are shown in little drawings. Museums, parks and other attractions are also shown. The pictures make it easy to recognise places on the map and also in real life, when you get there.

With a tourist map, you can find your way around a city, even without a guide!

Shakespeare's Globe Theatre is by the River Thames.

TRY THIS!

Look at the map opposite and fill in the blanks:

- The Monument is near ... Bridge.
- The *Golden Hinde* is close to the River ...
- A street called ... runs near the Tate Modern and Shakespeare's Globe Theatre.

COUNTRYSIDE MAPS

Jean Macdonald works as a ranger in a national park. She uses maps of the countryside every day at work, for example to find places or show information.

In Britain, countryside maps are made by the main mapping authority, Ordnance Survey (OS for short).

KEY
- † Church
- ✕ Windmill
- i Information
- Nature reserve
- Woodland
- Village
- Road
- River

Map symbols show a lot of information in a way that is easy to read. Always check the meaning of symbols in the key.

Map symbols

OS maps use signs called symbols instead of the little drawings used on tourist maps. Map symbols include letters, such as "i" for information centre. Coloured lines mark roads, rivers and railways. Some symbols are simple pictures. For example, a little picture of a bird can mean a nature reserve.

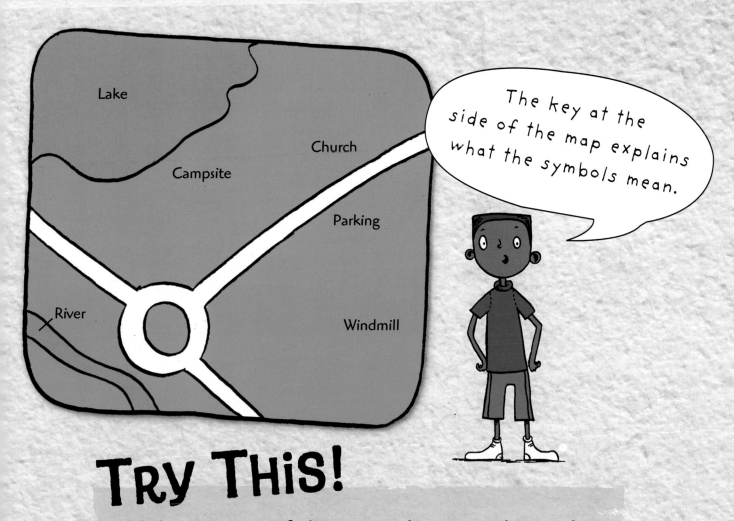

The key at the side of the map explains what the symbols mean.

TRY THIS!

Make a copy of the map above, without the words. Use symbols instead of words to show locations. If you don't know the symbol for a feature, you could make up your own.

A VET'S JOURNEY

Mrs Jenkins is a vet. She works in a town but also drives around the countryside, visiting farmers and pet owners.

Like many motorists, I use a road map to find my way on country roads.

Road maps show the information motorists need on journeys.

Road maps

Road maps help motorists to plan routes and find the way on journeys. Motorways, highways and small roads are shown as lines of different colours. Road numbers are given on the map and also on road signs, so drivers know which way to go.

Sat nav

Nowadays, many motorists use a satellite navigation system, or sat nav. The screen in your car is similar to a road map, but also shows your location. The map changes as you travel. The system also tells you which way to go.

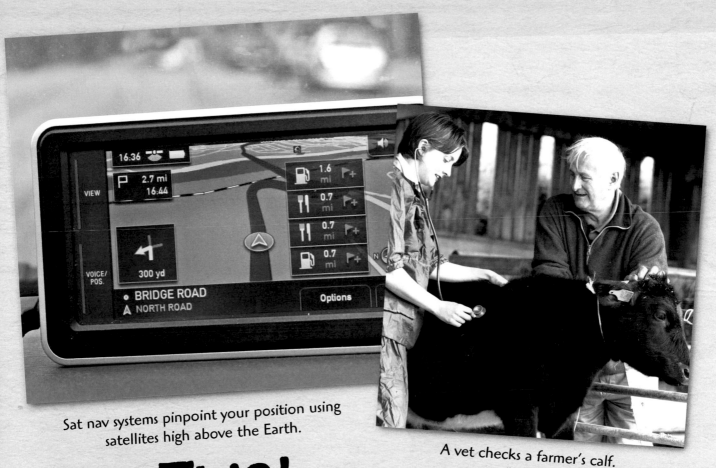

Sat nav systems pinpoint your position using satellites high above the Earth.

A vet checks a farmer's calf.

TRY THiS!

Road maps often show several ways to reach a location. Mrs Jenkins needs to drive from the vets' practice in Downside to Foxhole Farm. Look at the map opposite and work out two different ways to get there. Which route would you choose?

TRUCK DRIVER AND SCALE MAPS

Dai Evans is a truck driver. He drives between cities on motorways, and then finds his way through narrow city streets to deliver his load.

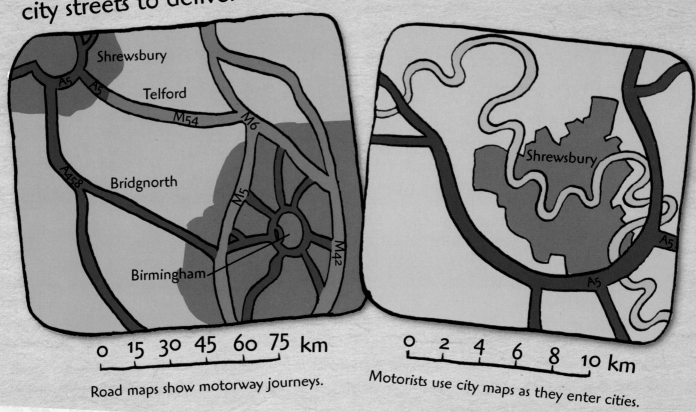

Road maps show motorway journeys.

Motorists use city maps as they enter cities.

Scale and size

On motorways, Dai uses road maps to check his route. These maps show a large area, but with little detail. In towns, Dai uses street maps, which show a small area in detail. Road and street maps have different scales – the scale is the size the map is drawn to.

The scale of the map is shown in the scale bar. On many road maps, 1 centimetre on the map stands for 10 or 20 kilometres in real life. On many street maps, 1 centimetre stands for 0.5 kilometre. Knowing the map's scale can help you work out how long your journey will take.

I use a street map to find the delivery location.

A street map of Shrewsbury.

TRY THIS!

Practise using maps of different scales on the Internet. Find a map of your area by logging on to https://maps. google.co.uk/. Use the zooming tool to change the scale of the map and make it larger or smaller.

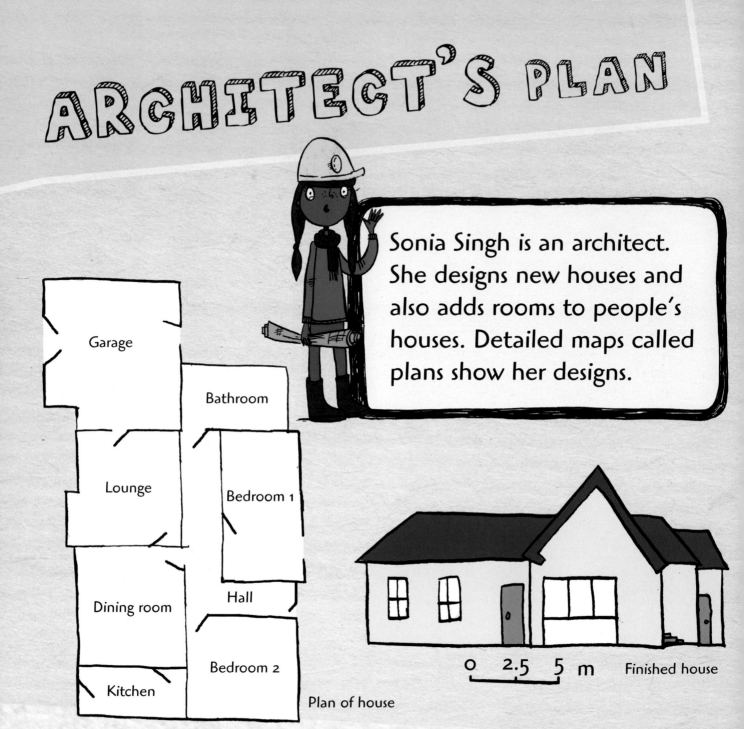

Sonia Singh is an architect. She designs new houses and also adds rooms to people's houses. Detailed maps called plans show her designs.

Garage

Bathroom

Lounge

Bedroom 1

Dining room

Hall

Bedroom 2

Kitchen

Plan of house

0   2.5   5 m

Finished house

Plan maps

Plans are very large-scale maps that show buildings in detail. The plan shows the size and shape of every room, and the position of doors and windows. Sonia adds a scale bar to show the scale. She shows the finished plan to the house owner and town planner to check everything is OK.

Bob Jones is a builder. He follows the architect's plan at every stage, from laying the foundations to building the walls and nailing on the roof.

I use the scale to work out how measurements on the map relate to the real measurements I make.

TRY THIS!

Make a plan of your bedroom. Measure the length and width of the room using a tape measure. Decide on a scale, such as 5 cm = 1 metre. Draw the outline on squared paper using a ruler. Measure and mark features such as a window, door and bed.

ICE CREAM VAN'S ROUTE

Mr Ali drives an ice cream van. The map below shows his route, as he drives through the streets and stops to sell ice creams.

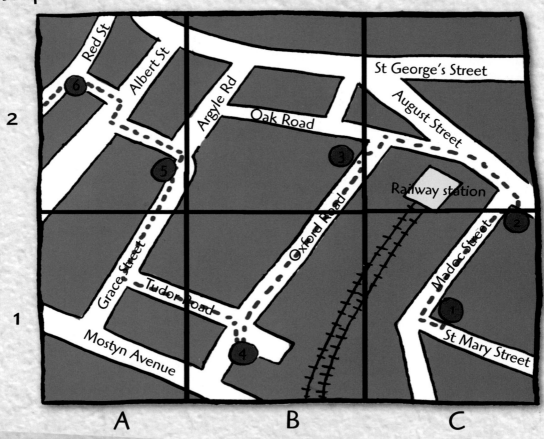

This map has a six-square grid.

Grid of squares

Maps like the one above are divided into squares. Lines running up and across the map form the squares. Look closely and you see that squares running across the map have letters, and ones running up have numbers.

Grid references

The letters and numbers give an exact location called a grid reference. The reference is always given in a certain order. Put your finger at the bottom left-hand corner of the map. Move it sideways to find a letter, then up to find a number. This gives a location such as square A2.

Ice cream rounds can cover a large area with many stops.

Grid references pinpoint locations such as the places I stop at to sell ice creams.

TRY THIS!

Look at the map opposite and answer these questions:

- Which number stop does Mr Ali make in square B2?
- Give the grid reference for Mr Ali's fourth stop.

LAND USE AT THE ZOO

Jane Fox is a zookeeper. She looks after large African animals, such as giraffes and elephants. Her fellow keepers, Bill, Mike and Sarah, look after other types of animals, such as big cats, reptiles and birds.

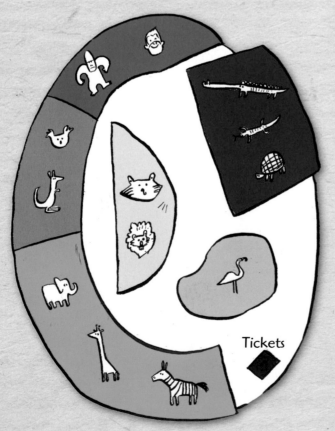

KEY

- Monkey world
- Australian Outback
- African savannah
- Big cats
- Reptile house
- Waterbirds

Tickets

Feeding time at the zoo

Land use maps

The map opposite shows Jane's zoo. The pens with different groups of animals are shown in different colours. The colours make it very easy to find the animals you want to visit. Maps that show how areas are used are called land use maps.

Land use maps of different scales show how land is used in a whole region, city, zoo or just a building, like the map here.

Way to zoo

Displays about zoo animals

KEY
7 — Door
☕ — Café
🚹🚺 — Toilets
🎁 — Shop

Entrance

Tickets

TRY THIS!

Make a land use map of your garden or a friend's garden. Show areas such as grass, decking, concrete, flowerbeds and trees in different colours. Add a key to explain the colours.

CAPTAIN AND COMPASS

Captain Cod is a ferry boat captain. He steers his boat across the sea and into harbour. Out to sea, there are no landmarks. Sailors steer using compass directions. North, south, east and west are the four main compass directions.

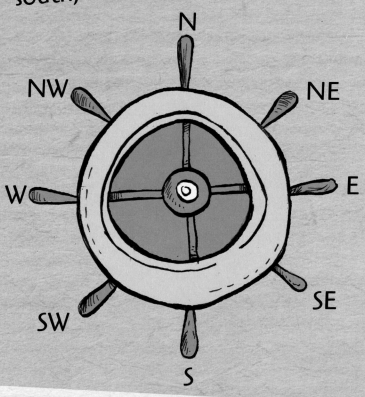

In between the four main compass points are four more points: northeast, southeast, southwest and northwest.

Using a compass

You can use a compass to find your way on land as well as at sea. The red magnetic compass needle always points north. You can use this to work out which way you are facing. Most maps show compass directions. North is usually at the top of the map.

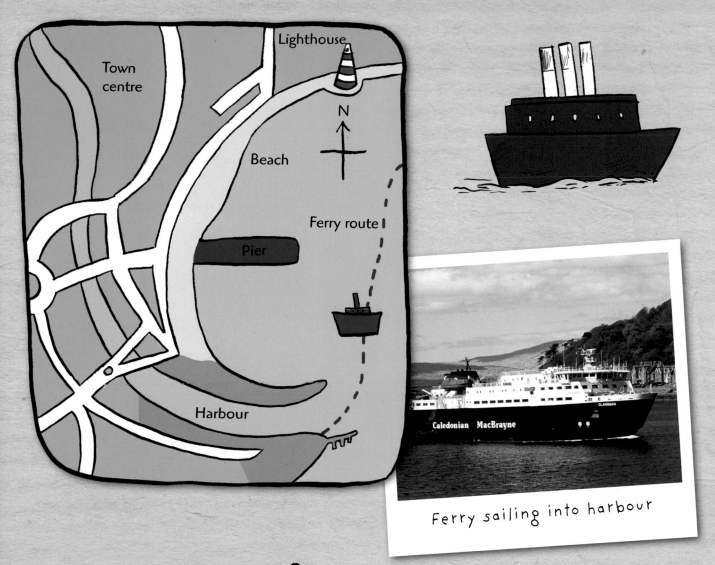

Ferry sailing into harbour

TRY THIS!

Compass directions allow you to locate places on maps and in real life in relation to one another. For example, on the map above, the pier is southwest of the lighthouse. Now answer these questions:

• What feature is north of the harbour?
• In which direction would you walk to get from the pier to the town centre?

PLUMBER'S MAP

Mr Cox is a plumber. He fixes leaks and builds new showers, baths and toilets in people's houses. Before he adds any new plumbing, he studies a plan map of the house.

KEY

Pipes

Pipes and cables

Architects' plans often show the location of water pipes and electric cables. That way, plumbers and electricians can do their work without fear of damaging existing pipes or cables.

Plan maps that use colour to show electricity or water supply do two jobs — they act as a plan and land use map rolled into one.

KEY

Door

Wash basin

Toilet

Stairs

Ground floor

Back door

Lounge

Kitchen

Hall

Washing machine

First floor

Bath

Bedroom 1

Bedroom 2

Bedroom 3

This plan shows water supply in a house.

TRY THIS!

How many rooms in your house are supplied with water? Make a simple plan of your house. If there are several floors, make a separate plan of each. Colour any rooms that are supplied with water blue. You could add symbols to show features such as a shower, toilet, bath and sink.

MOUNTAIN MAPS

Cathy Field works as a mountain guide. She leads walks to the summit of hills and then back down to the valley.

> My walks are steep, but it's hard to show steepness on the flat surface of a map.

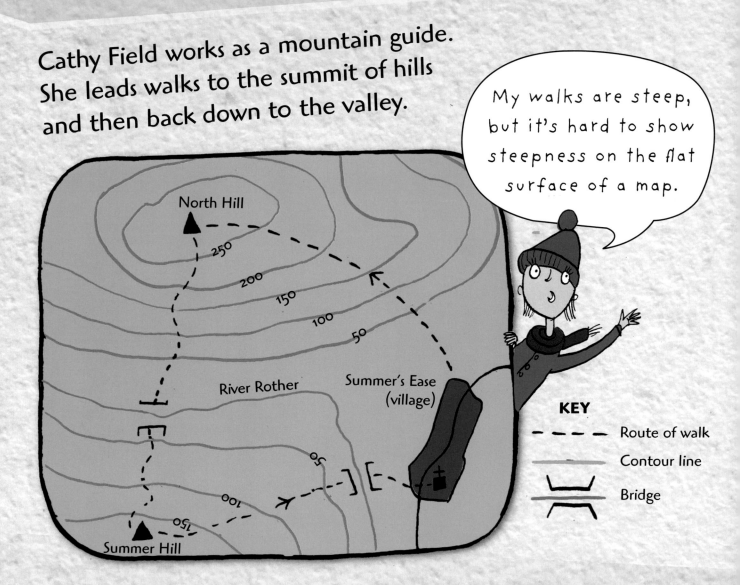

North Hill

250

200

150

100

50

River Rother

Summer's Ease (village)

50

100

50

100

150

Summer Hill

KEY

– – – – – Route of walk

———— Contour line

Bridge

Showing mountains

Many maps show hills and mountains using lines called contours. These faint lines link places at the same height above sea level. Numbers on the lines give the height in metres. The numbers always face uphill, so you know if the land is rising or falling.

On some maps the height of the land is shown in colours. Mountains are usually brown or purple, valleys and lowlands are green or yellow.

KEY

Above 800 m

500–800 m

Below 500 m

Solway Firth

Skiddaw
931 m

Helvellyn
950 m

Scafell Pike
978 m

Irish Sea

This map shows the English Lake District.

Mountain with steep sides

TRY THIS!

The map opposite shows Cathy's walk. Look at the map and fill in the blanks:

- The highest point of the walk is ...
- The total height climbed on the walk is ...
- The total height lost on the walk is ...

SIGNS OF THE PAST

Miss Taylor is a history teacher. She takes her class on field trips to explore historic places such as castles, forts and battlefields. Miss Taylor says being a history teacher is like being a detective!

Signs of the past are all around us, but the clues are often hidden, so you have to know where to look.

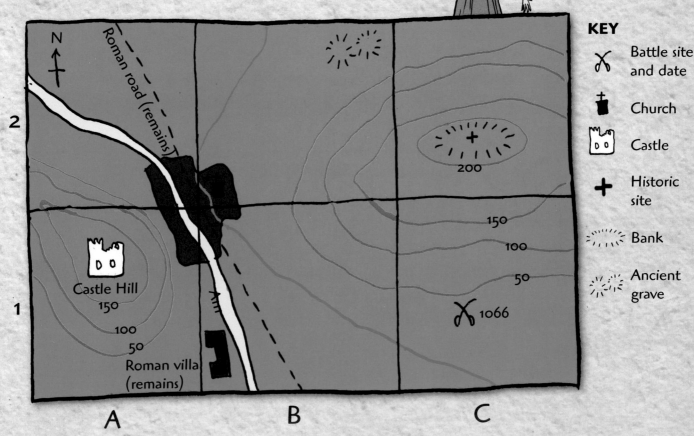

KEY

⚔ Battle site and date

⛪ Church

🏰 Castle

✚ Historic site

Bank

Ancient grave

Roman road (remains)

N

2

Castle Hill
150
100
50
Roman villa (remains)

200

150
100
50
⚔ 1066

1

A   B   C

Miss Taylor's map shows an area with many historic sites.

Old maps

Historic sites such as castles, forts and stone circles are marked on many maps. The key shows the new symbols. Miss Taylor also studies old maps to learn about history. In past times, people drew maps from high points such as towers. Nowadays, we use pictures taken by planes or satellites high above the landscape.

Old maps give clues about history, but they aren't always as accurate as modern maps.

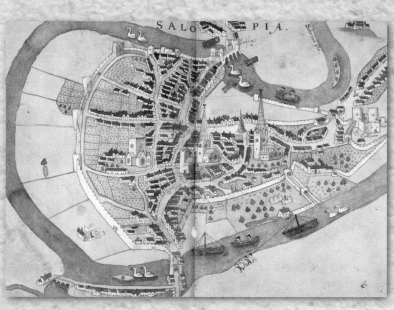

A old map of Shrewsbury.

TRY THIS!

Look at Miss Taylor's map. You'll need all the map skills in this book to answer these questions!

- Give the height of the bank in square C2.
- What historic site can be found in square A2?
- Give the grid ref for the castle. Find the symbol in the key.

What the words mean

Accurate Of something that is correct or right.

Aerial view A view from above.

Architect A person who designs buildings

Compass A tool that shows directions and helps you find your way.

Compass rose A symbol that shows compass directions.

Grid Squares on a map made by lines running up, down and across the page.

Grid reference Directions provided by the grid on a map.

Land use map A map that shows what land or buildings are used for.

Locate To find.

Key A panel on a map that shows the meaning of symbols.

Plan A map that shows a small area, such as a building or room.

Road map A map of a large area that shows roads, and is useful on journeys.

Scale The size a map is drawn to.

Street map A map of a town or village that gives the names of streets.

Symbol A sign or picture that stands for something in real life.

More information

Books

Marta Segal Block and
Daniel R Block,
Reading Maps
(Heinemann, 2008)

Sally Hewitt,
Project Geography: Maps
(Franklin Watts, 2013)

Ruth Nason,
Where People Work
(Franklin Watts, 2010)

Websites

Mapskills (PowerPoint) – Think Geography

www.thinkgeography.org.uk/Year%20
8%20Geog/.../Mapskills.ppt
This site explains map skills and
has lots of exercises to practise
your map skills.

Ordnance Survey: Map reading made easy

http://mapzone ordnancesurvey co.uk/
mapzone/PagesHomeworkHelp/docs/
easypeasy.pdf
Download this handy guide
to map reading.

BBC – GCSE Bitesize: Basics of mapping: 1

www.bbc.co.uk/schools/gcsebitesize/
geography/geographical_skills/maps_
rev1.shtml
A summary of map reading
skills for pupils learning
geography at school.

Index

Titles in the series:

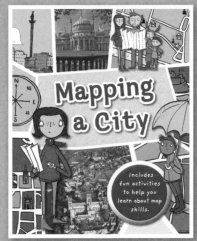

9780750285742

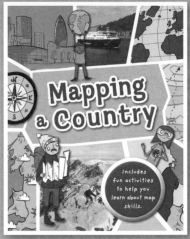

9780750285735

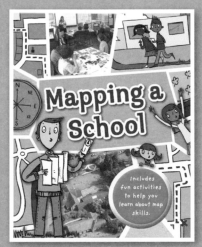

9780750285780

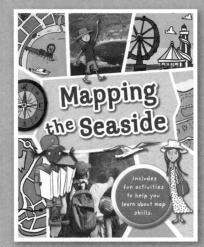

9780750285773

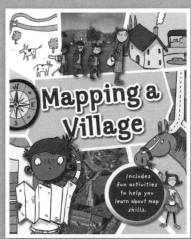

9780750285728

9780750285766